Nicky and the Bumble Bee

RUTH KIRTLEY

Illustrated by Linda Bir

Scripture Union
130 City Road, London EC1V 2NJ

By the same author
Nicky's Shadow

© Ruth Kirtley 1989
First published 1989

ISBN 0 86201 566 9

Phototypeset by Input Typesetting Ltd., London
Printed and bound in Great Britain by Cox and Wyman Ltd., Reading

Nicky and the
Bumble Bee

Contents

The runner bean race

Nicky is really Nicholas, but hardly anyone ever calls him by that name. He's quite an ordinary boy, really, with curly brown hair and freckles on his nose. He's not thin but not fat either and he's getting quite tall. His big brother Martin is nine and he's very tall, with curly ginger hair like Daddy. Sometimes he teases Nicky but they're good friends really.

When Nicky gets impatient about being the smallest in the family Mummy says she's sure he'll be tall like Daddy one day and anyway it's nice to have someone else who's short to keep her company for a while!

Nicky's a busy boy, always doing things. He likes digging holes in the back garden and riding his bike. He's interested in 'finding out' and of course he plays with his special friends Edward, Charlene and Stefan. These stories are about some of the things that happened to Nicky when he was five and had started school.

One afternoon in spring Mrs Lawson told Nicky's class that they were going to do some planting. They had been learning about seeds and how they grow, looking at different shapes, sizes and colours, and Mrs Lawson had explained how seeds grew into different plants. The children had tried to guess what kind of plant each seed would grow into and now each table was having a turn at planting some seeds of their own. It was exciting and they could hardly wait to start. Mrs Lawson had to say, 'Quiet children, *quiet!*' rather a lot of times.

Red table planted tiny orangey-brown cress seeds. Yellow table had black and white striped sunflower seeds, then blue table had round, whitish, knobbly nasturtium seeds and last of all, Nicky's table, which was green table, had runner beans. There were five other children on green table with Nicky and one of those was Charlene. She was one of Nicky's old play-group friends.

When it was green table's turn Mrs Lawson gave each child a large plastic flowerpot and they had to scoop special crumbly black earth out of a big sack on the floor. The table was covered in newspapers and the children all wore their painting aprons. 'Try not to spill *too* much earth,' said Mrs Lawson and they did try, very hard, though it wasn't easy. At last their pots were full to the brim.

Then Mrs Lawson gave each of them a runner bean seed. 'Have a good look at them,' she said. 'Tell me what you see.' The children studied their seeds carefully, squeezing and sniffing them. Edward even tried biting his! Then they began to talk about them and Mrs Lawson listened and wrote down on a big sheet of paper some of the words they used.

'They're quite big,' said Charlene. 'Bigger than cress seeds.'

'And hard,' said someone else.

'They're black with pink speckles,' said Nicky.

'*No* pink with black speckles,' another boy said.

When they had finished looking and talking each child made a hole in the soil with a finger and gently pressed their bean seeds into it.

'Why do we need such *big* pots?' Nicky wanted to

know. 'Our seeds will get lost in these big pots.'

'Ah, you wait!' said Mrs Lawson with a mysterious smile. 'Your seeds have big pots for a good reason. Now cover up your seeds and don't forget to water them.' Last of all each of them wrote their name on a label and stuck it on their flowerpot, and then the flowerpots were put on the classroom window sill with all the others. 'You won't see anything happening for a little while,' Mrs Lawson warned them, but, even so, Nicky was a bit disappointed when, next day, the soil in his flowerpot looked just the same. He'd half expected to see *something* growing there!

The days passed and the children forgot about the seeds – there was so much else to do. Then, one day, red table had a surprise. 'Miss! Miss!' shouted the children. 'Our seeds are coming up!' And, sure enough, they were. There were tiny white shoots just breaking out of the brown skin of the cress seeds. Red table were very pleased. All the other flowerpots still looked very boring. Each day the cress grew taller and greener and gradually, too, some of the seeds in the other pots began to sprout. Up came the nasturtiums and the sunflowers; thicker and greener than the cress and some with the old seedskin still sticking to the tiny leaves, like a funny little hat.

Green table were disappointed. 'Our seeds were the quickest!' boasted red table. 'Our seeds are taller,' said yellow table.

Nicky and his table looked glum. 'Be patient,' smiled Mrs Lawson. 'They'll come up soon.'

More days passed and, apart from when they watered their seeds, Nicky's table almost forgot about them. The cress seeds grew and were cut and made into egg and cress sandwiches for red table. The sunflowers grew bigger and greener and then, one Monday morning, hooray! there were the runner beans – through at last. Strong, green shoots with small crinkled leaves were sprouting from each pot. At *last* there was something to see! Now green table hardly noticed the other children's plants. They watched only their own as, day by day, they grew tall and straight. 'Now do you see why you needed such big flowerpots?' said Mrs Lawson.

'Mine's the tallest,' said Nicky one day.

'No, *mine* is!'

'It's mine!' They all argued happily.

'Let's have a race,' suggested Charlene. 'Yes! The first one to touch the ceiling!' The others agreed but, long before the plants reached the ceiling, they began to flop over and grow out sideways.

'What's the matter?' said Nicky in great alarm. 'They're not going up any more!'

'Don't worry,' Mrs Lawson said calmly. 'They're just telling us that it's time they had something to hold on to. Their stems aren't as strong as the sunflowers and they don't creep along the ground like the nasturtiums.' Next day she brought some thin sticks and when the children pushed one into each pot their plants soon began to twist and turn neatly around and up the sticks, and the runner bean race went on.

'I'm the winner,' Charlene announced firmly one day. 'My plant has run out of stick. Look, it's twisting about in the air.' The rest of the green table had to agree that Charlene's bean had won the race, but only just. The others weren't far behind.

Then it was time for the school holidays. 'Your plants are too big for the classroom now,' said Mrs Lawson. 'I think it's time to take them home and put them into the garden or a bigger flowerpot.' So, all the plants went

home, except for the cress, of course, because that had already been eaten!

Nicky proudly showed his plant to Mummy and Daddy, and Martin. 'It's *lovely*,' said Mummy. 'Look, it's got red flowers on it.'

'When can we *eat* them?' asked Martin.

Daddy helped Nicky to plant his runner bean in the garden, beside a wire fence, so that it had something to hold on to. Soon the red flowers were gone and tiny green beans took their place. All through the summer Nicky carefully watered his plant and now and then he stood beside it while Daddy measured it. The plant grew taller and taller, far above Nicky's head and even higher than Daddy's.

At last the beans were big enough to pick. Carefully Nicky snapped them off their stalks, searching behind leaves and crouching down and looking underneath to make sure he didn't miss any. Mummy was very pleased when he brought in a big handful of lovely green beans.

'I'll cook them for dinner,' she promised. Nicky helped her to wash and slice them. One bean was bigger and fatter than the others. Inside were several bright pink bean seeds.

'They're like the one I planted,' said Nicky. He looked at them and at the pan of sliced beans and he thought about the tall green plant in the garden. 'All these beans from just one bean seed,' he said. 'Not just one bean grows – you get lots!' He thought a bit more. 'Mummy, if I planted these new pink beans, would I get *more* plants and more beans?'

'Mmm, I expect so,' Mummy answered.

'Then I'd have lots and lots and lots and *lots* of beans!' Nicky's eyes were round and shiny at the thought.

'Yes, that's how it works,' Mummy said. 'From one

bean seed God gives us lots more. Now move out of the way while I put these on to cook.'

Nicky watched as Mummy put the pan of beans on to cook. 'That was a clever idea of God's, to think of that, wasn't it?' he said. Then he went off to have another look at his plant, just to make *quite* sure he hadn't missed any beans!

Nicky and the bumble bee

One morning at school Nicky was very busy. He and Edward, his best friend, were sitting together, drawing a picture in their Busy Books about the puppet show that had visited the school the day before. All the children were busy, doing this and that, and there was a hum of busyness in the classroom – not too loud, but not quiet either.

Nicky was drawing a picture of the clown puppet, who drove a funny old blue car. The clown had sung a song about his old car and he'd asked the children to sing with him and bounce up and down, as if they were riding in the car, too. Nicky had liked that part of the puppet show best of all. Edward's picture was of the policeman puppet who told them all how to cross the road safely. Nicky and Edward had been working away for a while when Nicky saw, out of the corner of his eye, that his friend Charlene was playing with the construction set. Nicky put down his blue crayon and watched. Charlene was making a car. I'd like to do that, thought Nicky and he slid off his chair and joined Charlene at her table.

'You can help,' she said, so Nicky began to build a garage or a house or something with a roof. He hadn't decided what it was.

Suddenly Mrs Lawson called across the room, 'Nicky! What are you doing over there? Have you finished your Busy Book work?'

'No, Mrs Lawson.'

'Well, come along then! Charlene has finished her work, that's why she's playing. When you've finished you can play too.' Nicky sighed and went back to his chair. Edward had finished his policeman picture and now he was writing his story. Mrs Lawson had written it down and he was copying underneath. It was very neat.

Nicky huffed and puffed to himself and scribbled away with a red crayon. That'll do, he thought to himself. Then he told his story to Mrs Lawson and she wrote the words for him. Back at his table, Nicky grabbed a pencil and began to copy Mrs Lawson's printing. Edward was still writing, slowly and carefully, and humming quietly to himself. Now and again Nicky looked over to where Charlene was playing.

Scribble, scribble, scribble, finished! Nicky dashed over to Mrs Lawson who was arranging jars of flowers on the Nature Table with a group of children. 'I've done it! Can I play now?' Mrs Lawson looked at the book and then at Nicky.

'Oh, *Nicky*! What's happened to your writing?' Nicky screwed up his mouth and looked down at his feet. 'You don't want Mummy and Daddy to see this messy work, do you? Now, turn the page and we'll start again.'

'But I want to do construction,' said Nicky sadly.

'There's *plenty* of time for that later. There's no need to rush. Don't spoil your whole book by being in a hurry. Go and do it slowly this time!'

Back went Nicky to his chair and this time he tried very hard to write more slowly and carefully. It wasn't easy when so many other children seemed to be finishing. Hmm, yes, but it *does* look better this time, thought Nicky as he went to show Mrs Lawson.

'That's *much* better!' she said with a smile. 'Off you go, Speedy, and don't be in such a rush next time!'

At home Nicky sometimes had the same problem. He would do things in a hurry, and then find that he had to do them again. 'Tidy up the Lego before tea, please,' said Mummy. Well some of it went back in the box, but the rest was pushed under the armchair. Mummy found it next day when she vacuumed the carpet. 'Do it again, *properly*,' she said.

Daddy was weeding the garden. 'Take these weeds to the compost heap, there's a good boy,' he said. Nicky was playing with his little cars. He didn't really want to stop. He grabbed the bucket of weeds, ran half-way up the garden and tipped them out behind a bush. Daddy wasn't very pleased when he found them later!

One Saturday Nicky was in the garden again, riding his bike round and round the grass. He had decided that he would do ten circuits of the grass without stopping. Mummy called from the back door.

'Nicky! Come in here a minute!' Nicky wobbled and almost fell off. Bother! He'd lost count, too. He dropped his bike on the grass and sighed to himself as he trotted over to the house.

In the kitchen Mummy showed him the birthday card she'd bought for Grannie. It was Grannie's birthday the next day and they were going to have a special birthday tea with red jelly and cake.

'Come and write your name on Grannie's card,' said Mummy. She and Daddy and Martin had already written theirs but there was a big space left for his name. He took the pencil that Mummy held out to him and scribbled quickly. Mummy glanced over his shoulder. 'Is that the best you can do?' she asked. 'I can hardly read it.'

Nicky shrugged his shoulders. He was in a hurry to get back outside again. 'Perhaps the pencil isn't sharp enough,' he suggested. Then he escaped to the garden before Mummy could think of anything to say.

He completed five circuits of the grass and then stopped to rest his aching knees. All this pedalling was rather tiring!

Bzz-zzz-zzz! What was that? Bzz-zzz-ZZZ! Nicky looked around him. Something was buzzing, but what was it and *where* was it? There were some tall plants in a border nearby. Some of them reached up above Nicky's head. They were foxgloves, tall and straight with rows of pink flowers up the stem. Nicky and Martin used to put the long, pink flowers on their fingers, when they fell from the stems. They were more like funny pink hats than gloves. Bzz-zzz-zzz! Nicky went close to the tall plants and then jumped as a fat, fluffy bee tumbled backwards out of one of the flowers.

'Oh!' laughed Nicky. 'You gave me a surprise!' The bee buzzed away, leaving the tall stem nodding gently. Almost at once it was back, landing on a pink spotted flower and pushing its way inside again. Was it the same bee? It certainly looked the same but it was hard to tell.

Nicky crept closer to the flowers again and peered inside. He couldn't see very much but there was a lot of buzzing going on. Standing still and listening Nicky realised that there was a humming sound all around him. There were bees busily flying in and out of the flowers all along the border. It reminded him of the busy hum in the classroom at school!

'What are you watching, Nicky?' asked Daddy as he

came past with the wheelbarrow.

'The bees,' Nicky replied. 'They're working *so* hard!' Nicky and Daddy watched together for a while. 'They keep coming back,' said Nicky. 'When will they finish?'

'Oh, not until tonight,' Daddy replied. 'It's their job, you see. That's what they do all day. They won't stop until they've collected all the nectar they need.'

'I'd be bored!' said Nicky.

'That's because you're not a bee!' Daddy laughed. 'But if you *were* a bee you'd be in trouble if you didn't do your job properly!' Nicky grinned and his face turned rather pink. He was remembering the Lego and the pile of weeds behind the bush. 'God made the bees to do their job and they have to do it properly,' Daddy explained. 'Otherwise there won't be enough food for themselves or their babies. God wants us to do our work well - the best we can. That makes him glad and other people too. It's quicker in the end, as well, because you don't have to keep doing things again.' Daddy poked Nicky in the tummy with his finger as he said this.

Nicky giggled and grabbed Daddy's finger. 'I'm a busy, buzzy bee and I'll sting you if you poke me!' He buzzed across the garden and into the house. He'd had an idea and he wanted to get to work straight away!

Ten minutes later Daddy came into the kitchen for his coffee and found Nicky sitting drinking some orange juice and eating a biscuit. On the table lay Grannie's birthday card, a pencil and a large green rubber. Mummy picked up the card and pointed to Nicky's name, printed neat and clear this time, and with three big X's underneath. Nicky smiled proudly over the top of his mug.

'Well done, buzzy bee!' said Daddy.

Nicky and the garden sprinkler

'Phew, I'm *hot*!' It was home-time and Nicky walked slowly across the playground to the school gate. He was trying to hold his reading book and lunch-box as well as his jumper, which kept dangling down and tripping him up. It had been very hot all day and now the afternoon sun shone down on the back of his head. Heat shimmered off the playground and made him screw up his eyes.

Mummy was waiting at the gate. 'I'm thirsty,' he complained, as she sorted out his bundle.

'We'll have a drink as soon as we get home,' Mummy promised. They went round to the gate where the big children came out and tried to find some shade by a wall. A bell rang and before long Martin pushed his way through the crowd of mothers, children and pushchairs. His face was red and shining and his hair stuck to his forehead. 'Martin, take your jacket off, you'll melt!' Mummy laughed. At last they were sorted out and set off for home. Nicky's friend Edward came too. He was staying for tea.

All the way home, which wasn't very far really, the boys puffed and panted and complained about the heat. Martin wanted to take his shirt off, Nicky said his hands were too hot to hold his lunch-box, Edward wanted an ice lolly. 'My goodness!' said Mummy. 'This is the first really hot day of the summer and all you do is moan. Would you rather it was raining like it did last week and we had to wear our wellies?'

'No,' sighed Martin. 'It's just that my school clothes feel all hot and tickly.'

Soon Mummy was loaded up with all the things the boys said they couldn't carry, and they all crept along, keeping in the shade of fences and hedges. Martin put his jumper on his head to make a sun hat and Nicky fanned himself with his reading book. When they arrived home the boys flopped on the grass in the back garden while Mummy quickly made cold drinks for everyone. Nicky helped to carry some of them outside. The ice-cubes tinkled together as they floated in the top of each mug.

'Ooooh, *lovely*!' sighed Edward after several sips.

Nicky held his mug against his hot forehead and smiled. 'Nice and cool!' he said. He and Edward watched lazily as Martin gulped down his drink and then hurried across to the garden shed. 'Crash! Thud! Clunk!' What was Martin up to now? Surely it was too hot to do *anything*?

Suddenly Martin burst out of the shed, dragging something long and heavy behind him. The garden hose! 'Can we use this, Mum?' he shouted.

'Yes, yes, yes! Let's have the hose!' shouted Nicky and Edward.

'All right,' agreed Mummy. 'We'll fit the sprinkler on the end and then you can water the garden as well as cool yourselves off.' She and Martin fixed the sprinkler on and then ran the hose down the garden to the tap by the kitchen door.

'Stand by, ready for action!' shouted Martin, with his

hand on the tap.

'Wait!' shouted Mummy. 'Don't forget to take your clothes off!'

At last they were ready. The boys waited impatiently beside the sprinkler while Mummy turned the tap. 'Five, four, three, two one, zero – here it comes!' she called. There was a faint hissing from the tap, the hose jerked and twisted as if it was a huge snake, then with a sudden splutter the sprinkler came to life! A spray of silver drops shot into the air, shimmering and sparkling in the sunlight. The boys shrieked with delight. They danced under the spray, leapt through it or stood with their heads back and their mouths open, trying to catch the drops as they tickled their faces. It felt wonderful. Soon the hot stickiness of the day had been washed away and they were dripping wet.

'It's a good thing we remembered to take our clothes off,' said Edward solemnly. 'My mum would've been a bit cross if I went home all wet.'

After a while Mummy turned the sprinkler off because the grass was turning to mud. No one really minded though, because now they felt cool and ready to do other things. When they were dry and dressed again Martin helped Mummy to drag the hose to the vegetable garden and then they turned it on and left it to water the plants there.

'The plants are thirsty too,' said Edward as they stood watching the first drops fall blackly on the dry earth.

'They want a drink but they don't want to play like we did!' laughed Nicky.

'Plants die if you don't water them,' said Martin. He knew about things like that.

'So would we,' Mummy added. 'We all need water.'

'Some countries don't have enough water because they don't get much rain,' Martin continued. He was learning

22

about other countries at school.

'Well, why don't they just get some water out of the tap?' asked Nicky.

'They sometimes don't *have* taps, silly!' snorted Martin. 'Or just one for everyone to share.'

'That's right,' said Mummy. 'In some places the mummies have to walk a long, long way to get water in a bucket from a muddy hole.'

'I saw that on telly once,' said Edward.

Nicky shuddered and his eyes grew round. No tap? Muddy water to drink? Yuk!

'We need water for so many things,' said Mummy.

'Like drinks!' said Edward quickly.

'Baths!' said Nicky.

'The swimming pool!' Martin added.

'If there was hardly any water we'd all be very dirty, very hungry and *very* thirsty,' Mummy pointed out. 'That's why we really shouldn't moan about the rain – some people would love a really wet day because they feel hot and thirsty like we did today, all the time.'

After they had played for a while with Martin's new cricket set the boys all lay on their tummies on the grass and watched the sprinkler. The earth in the vegetable patch had turned dark and puddly and there was a nice fresh smell. Drops of water hung shining from the leaves and branches or pattered down somewhere out of sight.

'I'm glad we don't live in a hot country,' said Edward. 'I quite like the rain sometimes.'

'Today was hot but we had drinks and ice to make us cool,' said Martin.

'And the sprinkler,' said Nicky. 'That was good too.'

They lay thinking and watching and all the time the sprinkler kept turning, back and forth, back and forth, and the water sparkled in the sunlight.

The rainbow

There was bustle and noise at Nicky's house one Saturday morning. Daddy was hurrying up and down stairs saying, 'Where's my new shirt? Where's my striped tie?' and 'Who's moved my car keys?' Mummy was spending a long time in the bathroom and bedroom, in between trying to find things for Daddy and answering Nicky and Martin's questions.

Nicky and Martin were sitting on the stairs, getting in the way and watching what was going on. 'Why can't we go to the wedding too?' Nicky asked as Daddy stepped over him on his way downstairs.

'Because weddings are boring for children. It's all standing about and talking.'

'What about the food bit?' Martin wanted to know. He thought food was very important.

'Oh yes,' Daddy answered from the hall cupboard. 'There will probably be nice food but you have to *wait* a long time for it. Oh, bother it, where are my *keys*?' Daddy dashed upstairs again and banged on the bathroom door.

Martin wandered off to find something to do, while Nicky slowly slid downstairs step by step, to the bottom. A big box, wrapped in beautiful silver and pink paper sat on the table by the front door. A present! Nicky *loved* presents. What could it be? He carefully picked it up and shook it gently. It didn't rattle. He tore a little flap on one of the corners and tried to see underneath. 'Nicky!' He jumped and nearly dropped the present. Mummy was coming downstairs. 'That's John and Annie's wedding present,' she said. 'Please don't spoil it.'

'What's inside?' asked Nicky.

'A salad bowl.'

A salad bowl! What a funny present, thought Nicky. I wouldn't want anything like that for a present.

Mummy was all ready in her new dress and hat. 'You look different,' said Nicky, and she laughed.

'I hope I look nice too!'

Nicky nodded. 'Mm, yes.' He'd never seen Mummy wearing a hat before, except for the woolly one she wore in winter. 'I want to come too,' he said.

'Honestly, Nicky, you and Martin wouldn't like it. You'll have much more fun with Grannie.' At that moment the front door bell went 'bing-bong' and there *was* Grannie – all smiles – with a bulging shopping bag.

'Sorry I'm a bit late, love,' she said. 'I thought I'd pop into the shop on the way. Just to get a few bits and pieces for today.' She winked at Nicky. 'My, *my*! You do look smart!' she went on. 'Now go and enjoy yourselves and don't worry about us, we've got plenty to keep us busy, eh Nicky?' Nicky grinned. He always liked Grannie looking after them.

At last the car keys were found and the torn flap in the parcel was mended. Then Mummy and Daddy were ready to go. Mummy called Nicky and Martin to her. 'Now, before we go I want you to promise you'll be good for Grannie. No nonsense, all right?' They nodded solemnly. 'Your Saturday sweets are on top of the fridge but you don't have them until your bedroom is tidy. Grannie will decide. Oh, and don't forget, Panda needs her tea at four o'clock. Will you remember all that?'

Nicky, Martin and Grannie waved goodbye. As the car turned the corner Nicky felt a wet splash on his cheek and another on his hand. 'Oh dear,' said Grannie. 'It's starting to rain. Come inside quickly.' They were hardly inside the door when the rain began to pour down and it became so dark that they had to put the lights on in the house.

Nicky stared out of the window at the shining pavements and the bouncing raindrops. He was annoyed. 'Why did it have to rain?' he grumbled. 'I wanted to go to the park and show you the new stunts I can do on my bike.'

Grannie smiled as she unpacked her shopping bag. 'Oh, it'll clear up, later. Come and help me unpack these things.' Nicky forgot the rain as he helped Grannie. She always brought 'a few bits and pieces' when she came to look after them. Today there were home-made jam tarts and a can of fizzy drink for Nicky and Martin, as well as a big bag of crisps and a carton of chocolate ripple ice-cream for lunch.

Once they had unpacked Grannie put the kettle on and got out her knitting bag. She had half a new school jumper for Martin that she wanted to measure against him. While she and Martin were busy Nicky found a plate and put the jam tarts on it. Then Grannie made hot orange and coffee and they all had what she called 'elevenses'. Martin, who was good at telling the time, pointed out that it was only half-past ten.

'I don't care!' chuckled Grannie, 'my tummy says it's time for "elevenses"!'

'So does mine,' agreed Nicky.

Outside the rain still poured down. 'Oh, dear, that poor bride,' said Grannie with a sigh. 'I do hope it clears up for the photos.'

'I want to go out,' said Nicky.

'Me too,' said Martin.

'Not yet, we'd get soaked,' Grannie replied.

'It's been raining and raining. I think it's going to rain for *ever*,' said Nicky gloomily.

'Don't you worry, my love,' said Grannie. 'It'll clear up. It won't go on for ever. It can't. Now, how about a game of Snap?' So they played three games of Snap and then they tried Happy Families but Nicky wasn't very good at that. Afterwards Grannie did some knitting and Martin went off to finish a picture for school.

Nicky wandered into the kitchen and his eye was caught by the Saturday sweets, on top of the fridge. His mouth watered. He just felt like that packet of chocolate drops! Maybe he'd have just one or two. Quietly, he tore the packet open and then popped a handful of chocolate drops into his mouth. Mmmm, delicious!

'Hey, Nick!' shouted Martin, who was working at the kitchen table. 'Mum said no sweets till we'd cleared up. We promised.'

Nicky swallowed quickly and put the half-empty packet back on top of the fridge. 'I forgot,' he said in a sticky voice.

'A promise is a promise,' said Grannie from the doorway. 'We should always keep our promises. People need to know they can depend on us to do what we said we'd do. It's very important.' Grannie looked a bit stern but Nicky noticed that her eyes were still twinkling. 'Upstairs both of you and get that room tidy. I'll be up in ten minutes – *then* you can have your sweets.'

Martin and Nicky scampered upstairs and set to work.

In less than ten minutes the floor was clear, the bunks were tidy and all the toys were back in the toy-box or on the shelves.

'Very good,' said Grannie. 'Here are your sweets but don't eat them *all* before lunch!'

All through lunch the rain went on falling; not so heavily now, but there were big puddles all along the garden path. 'It's still raining,' Nicky sighed gloomily.

Martin laughed. 'Perhaps we'd better start making a boat, like Noah!'

Grannie looked up from stacking dishes. 'I don't think you'll need to do that. What happened at the end of that story? Can you remember what God did?'

Nicky and Martin thought for a while. 'The rainbow!' shouted Nicky.

'God promised not to flood the world again,' added Martin.

Grannie nodded. 'That's right. God made a promise and when he makes a promise he keeps it. He made the rainbow to remind *us*, not himself. He doesn't forget, like *some* people!' She laughed and tapped Nicky on the head with her finger. Nicky thought of the Saturday sweets and grinned.

All at once the room became very bright. 'The sun's come out!' Martin called from the window. 'It's stopped raining. We can go out now!'

Nicky squeaked with excitement. 'Come on Grannie! Quick, before it rains again.'

And so, as fast as they could, they put on their coats and wellies, and the boys hurried out to the shed for their bikes. Grannie took her umbrella, too. 'I don't trust those grey clouds,' she said.

It was lovely to be outside at last and the boys whooshed along the pavements and through all the

puddles, to the park. There were more puddles at the park but these didn't stop Nicky showing his new stunts to Grannie. The sky grew dark again and they sheltered under a big tree as the rain began to fall. The shower didn't last long and it was soon followed by the sun again.

'Just the sort of weather for a rainbow,' said Grannie.

Then it was time to go home. Off they splashed with the sun taking turns to shine between the rain showers. Just as they came to the garden gate Martin called, 'There's one!' and pointed to the sky above the houses opposite. There was a beautiful rainbow, shining clearly against the grey clouds.

'Miaow!' Sitting on the doorstep was a very wet and cross Panda. She shook the raindrops from her whiskers and rubbed and wound herself around their legs. 'It's Panda's tea-time!' said Nicky. 'We promised to feed her.' So after the wet coats and wellies had been put away, Grannie helped the boys to feed Panda. 'We didn't forget *that* promise,' said Nicky.

It was long after tea when Mummy and Daddy came home.

'Oof! My feet!' said Mummy, as she flopped into a chair.

'We saved you some cake,' said Daddy. 'Have you got room for it?'

Of course they had! Nicky shared his icing with Grannie.

When Grannie went home to her house it was a lovely sunny evening. The birds were singing and the puddles were almost dry. 'I told you,' she said, as she kissed the boys. 'I told you it wouldn't rain for ever. God always keeps his promises!'

Grandad's shed

In the long school holidays Nicky and Martin went to stay for a week with their Auntie Liz. They both enjoyed going to Auntie Liz's house. It was big and old and untidy. Auntie Liz never told you to keep your feet off the furniture or not to bounce on the beds and she let you spread your jam or honey *very* thickly on your bread.

Auntie Liz was married to Uncle Mark and they had a baby called Daniel. Nearly everyone called him Danny but he called himself Dan-Dans. Nicky wasn't very interested in babies but sometimes Danny did funny things like rubbing his dinner in his hair and then Nicky would laugh. There was also a big, hairy dog called Rufus and six chickens with no names. Because it was in the country there were fields all round the house and trees to climb and a little stream to play in. But the best thing of all about staying with Auntie Liz and Uncle Mark was Grandad.

Grandad lived with Auntie Liz and Uncle Mark in his 'den' as he called it. It was a bedroom and a sitting-room all in one room and it was downstairs at the back of the house. 'To get the sun,' said Grandad. Nicky and Martin used to like visiting Grandad in his den. He had his own television and his own kettle and he sometimes made them mugs of hot orange or cocoa while they watched the cricket.

Grandad also had a shed, a very special shed in the back garden, behind Uncle Mark's garage. Nicky and Martin weren't allowed in the shed by themselves. Indeed, the door had a big, heavy padlock on it and Grandad kept the key in his pocket.

It always gave Nicky an excited feeling when Grandad unlocked the padlock and creaked the door open. After climbing the step Nicky would close his eyes and sniff the special shed smell. Nowhere else smelled like Grandad's shed – a painty, woody, oily smell, all mixed up with other mysterious smells that Nicky didn't recognise. After the sniff Nicky would open his eyes and gaze about him at all the tools that hung neatly on the walls and the workbench with its sprinkling of sawdust, the jars of screws and tins of paint and old biscuit tins that were full of everything *except* biscuits!

It was a very interesting place and Nicky longed to be able to look in all the boxes and tins and touch the tools but Grandad had said he mustn't. 'They're not toys, you know.' he explained. 'Some of them are sharp and dangerous. You need to know how to use them.'

That's why he keeps the door locked, thought Nicky. If little Danny got in *he* might hurt himself.

One day, near the end of their stay, Nicky had nothing to do. He had climbed the trees, thrown sticks in the stream, talked to the chickens and now he felt bored. Martin was playing cricket with Uncle Mark and Auntie Liz was baking. Danny was asleep and Rufus was feeling hot and just lying on his side under a bush, panting. Half-way down the garden, in a sunny spot, Grandad was sitting in a deckchair reading the paper. He looked up as Nicky wandered past. 'Not playing cricket?' he asked.

'No,' sighed Nicky. 'They throw the ball too hard.'

'Got nothing to do?'

'No.'

'Nothing at all?'

'Well, I'd like something *different* to do.'

Slowly, Grandad folded his paper and then reached into his pocket. He took out a key.

'Come on, lad. You and me will just go and have a potter in the shed, shall we?'

Nicky's eyes lit up and he hopped and jumped round Grandad because he was so pleased. Down the garden they went. Rufus watched them go but he just thumped his tail on the ground and didn't follow. A ball whizzed over their heads and Uncle Mark's voice shouted, 'Not so *hard*, Martin! Remember the windows!'

Grandad unlocked the shed door. Creeeak! Mmm, there was the smell. Nicky shivered with pleasure and followed Grandad inside.

'Now,' said Grandad. 'I think you're old enough to be careful, aren't you, lad?' Nicky nodded his head solemnly. Grandad unhooked a small hammer and saw and reached down a jar of little nails. Then he pulled a box from under his work bench. It was full of pieces of wood, all different lengths and thicknesses. 'Off-cuts, these are,' he explained. Then he showed Nicky how to hold the hammer and nails and how to keep from hitting his fingers. He also showed him how to clamp the wood tight in the vice, so it wouldn't slip when you sawed it.

Nicky watched carefully as Grandad's hands moved this way and that. Grandad's hands were rough and brown with knobbly knuckles. There were hairs and darker brown patches on the backs of his hands.

'Your hands are very old, Grandad,' said Nicky.

Grandad chuckled. 'So's the rest of me, lad!'

Nicky put his small hand next to Grandad's larger one. His looked pink and podgy next to Grandad's. 'Your hands are so bumpy!'

'Ah, that's the arthritis. A proper nuisance, it is. But I still manage most things. Now, let's get to work.'

Nicky chose a piece of wood and started to hammer a nail into it. Bang! Bang! 'Oops! OW!' Nicky frowned at the crooked nail as he sucked his sore finger. 'You hammer *much* better than me, even with arther-itis,' he sighed.

'Not to worry, lad,' said Grandad. 'Just keep practising.' Then he settled himself on a stool at the end of the workbench and began to unscrew something at the back of an electric kettle.

'Your Auntie Liz has broken her kettle again. Forgot to put water in it, most likely.' They both worked together. Nicky was really enjoying himself. He hammered and sawed and Grandad didn't mind how many nails got bent. He just kept on working on the kettle and now and then he said helpful things like, 'Keep your fingers down a bit,' or 'That nail's too long for that thin piece of wood.' After a while Nicky found that the nails were going in straighter and, when he sawed, the edges of the wood weren't so raggy.

'Now I'm going to *make* something,' he announced. Grandad nodded, but kept on working. Nicky rummaged in the off-cuts box and found three pieces of wood almost the sizes he needed. The long, flat piece needed a bit taken off, so carefully he drew a line with the special soft-leaded pencil and then, with his tongue sticking out between his teeth, he began to saw.

Zzzip-zip, zzzip-zip, tap-tap, tap-tap-tap, bang, bang, BANG. Nicky worked away busily. At last he stopped. 'I've finished, Grandad, look!' He held up a little boat.

'Well, I never!' exclaimed Grandad. 'Now that's what I call a nice bit of work. Well done, Nicky lad!' Nicky beamed with pleasure as Grandad examined his boat. 'All it needs now is a spot of varnish,' said Grandad, 'Then it'll be ready for launching down at the stream.' He showed Nicky how to smooth the rough edges with scratchy sandpaper and then he opened a small can of something that made Nicky's nose prickle. 'This here's varnish. I think I'd better do this bit though. We don't want you going home with this stuff splashed on your clothes.' Slowly and carefully Grandad painted the varnish on. The little brush looked funny in his big hand but he was *so* neat. He didn't make one splash.

Later they walked back to the house. Nicky was proudly carrying his little boat on a piece of newspaper because the varnish wasn't quite dry. Grandad followed with the mended kettle. Nicky stopped and smiled. 'I've got lots of bumps today but I *made* something. That's good, isn't it, Grandad?'

Grandad nodded and he smiled too. 'It's wonderful to be able to make things and we've got wonderful hands to help us.' Nicky looked at his dirty hands with their bruised fingers.

'Mm, hands are useful things. Grandad . . .'

'Yes, lad?'

'Tomorrow, can we make a boat that's big enough for me and Martin to sail in?'

'We'll see,' said Grandad. And they went inside for tea.

New shoes

One day after school Mummy took Nicky and Martin to town shopping.

'Do we *have* to go to town?' sighed Nicky. He really wanted to go home and get on with a new hole he was digging behind the shed in the back garden.

'Yes, we do,' Mummy replied firmly. 'Martin's shoes are falling apart and we need to buy him some new ones.'

'They look all right,' said Nicky.

'They're not, though. Look!' Martin laughed as he hopped about on one foot and pointed to the sole of his shoe. 'See, there's nearly a hole here, and my toes are getting squashed, too.'

'Yes,' Mummy agreed as they hurried along the busy road. 'It's high time Martin had new shoes – his toes will grow crooked if they're squashed for too long.'

'And my feet will get wet soon, if it rains,' Martin added, hopping on the other foot for a change.

Nicky sighed and plodded along beside Mummy. 'Can I have new shoes, too?' he asked.

'Not yet, you still have plenty of space in yours,' said Mummy.

Nicky felt like arguing. '*Why* can't I have some?'

'Martin *needs* new shoes. He can't go to school in his socks! You'll have some when *you* need them.'

Nicky kicked an empty Coke can that was lying on the pavement. Clink! Bink! Clinkity-clink-clink-clink! It rolled and bounced along in front of him.

'Hey, pass it to me!' shouted Martin. He liked football. Nicky kicked the can hard and Martin darted across and began to dribble the can along the pavement. Nicky forgot about the shoes as he chased after Martin, leaving Mummy far behind. Back and forth across the pavement they went, dodging a pillar-box here and a lamppost there. Sometimes Martin passed to Nicky and he had a go at kicking but mostly Martin did the kicking and Nicky just ran.

Once the can rolled into the gutter and Martin jumped off the pavement to reach it.

'Careful!' called Mummy from behind. Clink! Binkity-clink-clank!

'It's a goal!' shouted Martin as the can shot into a shop doorway. The boys stopped, puffing and panting, at the pedestrian crossing as they waited for Mummy to catch up.

'Put it in the bin now,' she said. 'We've had enough of that noise.' Martin picked up the very dented can and dropped it into a rubbish bin nearby, then together they crossed the road.

Before going into the shoe shop they stopped and looked at the shoes in the window. 'I like those!' said Martin, pointing.

'You couldn't kick cans in those,' said Mummy. 'They don't look very strong.'

'How about these then?' Martin suggested.

'Mmm, we'll see,' was all Mummy would say.

Nicky leaned a hot cheek against the shop window. The glass was cool and he liked the feel of it. He huffed on it till a misty patch spread out and the rows of shoes inside almost seemed to disappear. Then he wrote a big N for Nicky in the misty patch with his finger and watched as it slowly faded away. Suddenly he felt Martin poking him. 'Come on, we're going inside!'

There were a lot of people waiting in the shoe shop. Nicky and Martin grew tired of sitting still and wandered about, looking at the different shoes on display. They giggled at the pink, fluffy slippers for girls. 'You'd look nice in those,' said Martin, teasing. Nicky pretended to be cross.

'No, I wouldn't. You'd look nice in *those*, Big Feet!' and he pointed to some enormous men's working boots with clumping soles and lots of laces.

At last it was Martin's turn and Nicky sat and watched while Martin's feet were measured. Then the sales girl talked to Mummy about what kind of shoes Martin should have, and then Martin told the sales girl what *he* thought he should have. The girl went away and came back with some boxes and took pair after pair of shoes out of their tissue paper wrappings for Martin to try on. One pair was too small, another pair wasn't suitable for school, but finally one pair was just right.

Nicky sat swinging his legs furiously and frowning at the floor. It wasn't *fair*! Why couldn't he have new shoes too? All the way home Martin skipped along in front twirling his shoe-shop bag.

Nicky was tired now and he walked quietly with Mummy, holding her hand. He told her what had happened at lunch-time that day, when one of the dinner ladies slipped on an apple core that someone had dropped. 'She nearly sat down!' said Nicky. 'Me and Charlene thought she would be cross, but she just laughed . . . Can we have spaghetti hoops for tea?'

When they arrived home it was tea-time and, while

Mummy was cooking, Martin tried on his new shoes. Then he clumped round the house, stopping now and then to look at himself in the long, hall mirror. He was very happy and really proud of his shiny new shoes. Nicky watched him for a while and then trailed off to the kitchen to find Mummy.

'What's the matter?' asked Mummy.

'Martin's showing off in his new shoes,' Nicky muttered. 'I wish *I* could have some.' He sighed and rubbed his eyes. He thought he might be going to cry.

'Oh, but Nicky, it's so nice getting new things,' Mummy said. 'I like it when I get something new – we all do. Come on, let's be happy with Martin, and then you'll feel better.' Nicky smiled a little smile.

Ker-lump, ker-lump, ker-lump. In came Martin. 'Hey Nick. I'll teach you how to tie shoe-laces on my new shoes.' Then Nicky smiled a bit more because he really wanted to learn how to do laces. He knelt down on the floor beside Martin to watch him tying and re-tying his new laces. 'Now you try, Nick,' he said and so Nicky tried.

They were busy for quite a while when Mummy suddenly said, 'Nicky, let me see your slippers please.' Nicky scrambled up and pit-patted across to Mummy. She picked up one of his feet and Nicky wobbled and hopped to keep his balance. 'Oh ho! Look what I've found,' said Mummy and she poked a finger through the toe of Nicky's slipper.

'Eee!' he squealed. 'That's my toe!'

'Yes,' laughed Mummy. 'There's a great big hole in the end of this slipper and it looks as though the other one's not much better. You know what this means, don't you?'

'New slippers!' shouted Nicky and Martin together.

Mummy nodded.

'I know just the kind of slippers that will suit Nicky,' said Martin, with a big grin.

Nicky leapt on Martin and together they rolled around the kitchen floor. '*Not* pink, fluffy ones!' shouted Nicky, and they all laughed.

Later that week Mummy bought Nicky a new pair of slippers. They weren't pink or fluffy, just a nice, plain, bright red. After that, everyone was happy.

The Christmas play

'Christmas is coming! Christmas is coming!' sang Nicky as he skipped home after school one afternoon. There were lots of things that told him Christmas was on its way. Suddenly, it seemed, the days were growing shorter and it was quite dark by tea-time. It was colder too, and Mummy had bought him and Martin new long trousers to wear to school. The woolly hats and mittens had come out from the top shelf of the hall cupboard, because some mornings it was quite frosty on the way to school. When they went to town the shop windows were bright with special Christmas displays, and there were colourful decorations on all the lampposts.

Nicky had helped Mummy to stir the Christmas pudding and cake mixtures, and he and Martin had written lists of things they would like for presents – just in case anyone should ask! But it was at school that things were really exciting. This was Nicky's first Christmas at school and he was enjoying it very much! Every day, after he'd done his writing and number work, there were interesting things to do. There were cards to make and sewing to finish and decorations to help with, and most exciting of all, there was the school concert.

Each class was doing something and at the end of term, right near Christmas, the parents had been invited to come and watch. Some classes were singing songs and acting out scenes showing how Christmas is celebrated in other countries, but Nicky's class had been chosen to do the Nativity play. Several times Mrs Lawson had read them the story of the first Christmas and now they all knew about how Mary was visited by the angel, how the shepherds and wise men had come to see the new Baby, and how Jesus was God's special present to the world that he loved so much. Then she picked some children to be the people in the story, others who were good readers to tell the story and the rest of the children were to sing the Christmas songs that went with the Christmas story.

At first Nicky had been rather disappointed not to be chosen to be someone like an inn-keeper or a shepherd, especially when he found out that they were going to dress up. 'I wish I could be someone in the play,' he said sadly. 'I'm only doing the singing. I'd like to dress up.'

'Oh, but you're very important!' Mummy had reassured him. 'Music and singing are a very special part of Christmas. You singers are just as important as the actors and the readers.'

'But no one will really *see* us,' explained Nicky.

'God will! You sing your very best and God will say, "Ah, there's my Nicky using that lovely voice I gave him"!'

Nicky giggled. 'That's funny!'

'Yes, but it's true, too! God loves to hear us praising him. You can do it at the concert, just as well as at Sunday School.'

Mrs Lawson had said the same sort of thing when they had begun to practise their play. 'Just because you aren't dressed up doesn't mean you're not needed. If the readers don't read nicely and the singers don't know all their words our audience won't understand our story. We must *all* do our best!'

So, now no one minded what they were doing because they each had an important part to play. Nicky worked hard, learning the words to all the songs. He even sang them in the bath! They were doing hardly any ordinary school work now, it was all cards and presents and decorations and practise, practise, practise for the concert. Soon the readers knew their words by heart and the actors knew exactly where to walk and stand without Mrs Lawson telling them. Nicky and the other singers knew their songs so well, they could have sung them in their sleep!

At last the day of the concert came. The school hall was decorated with paper chains and all the mums and dads and little brothers and sisters were squeezed in to watch. The children waited in their classrooms for their turns. They chattered excitedly while their teachers 'shushed' them. Nicky shivered with excitement as he gazed round at the shiny angel wings and the bright robes of the wise men. 'Our turn now,' called Mrs Lawson. 'Come *quietly*!' It was hard to be quiet when everything was so exciting. The children whispered and pushed and poked each other – they just couldn't help it!

Into the hall they came. Everyone knew where to stand but how strange it felt with all those faces, like pink blobs, staring at them. Nicky looked about him. Where were Mummy and Daddy? There was a shuffle and a rustle and the first reader stepped forward. 'One day a lady called Mary was visited by an angel . . .' They had begun! The words and movements came easily now, and when Mrs Lawson struck the note for the first song the children sang as loudly as they could. Mrs Lawson

beamed at them from the piano.

Half-way through 'Away in a Manger' Nicky suddenly spied Mummy and Daddy. He was so pleased that, for a moment, he forgot to sing. Then he gave them a huge smile, threw back his head and sang louder than ever.

When they finished the clapping was so loud it almost hurt their ears! 'That was *lovely*, children,' said Mrs Lawson when they were back in their classroom. Nicky bounced up and down with pleasure and he was still bouncing when Daddy and Mummy came to collect him. 'Well done, Nick,' said Daddy.

'We sang our *best*,' said bouncing Nicky. 'I like Christmas it's . . . *nice*!' He did one last, big bounce before he dashed off to find his coat. As they were hurrying home Nicky suddenly asked, 'Do you think God heard me singing?'

'I'm sure he did,' replied Mummy.

'Good,' said Nicky, 'because I was saying thank you to him. I was saying thank you for making Christmas,' and he zoomed off to catch up with Martin, singing at the top of his voice.

Changes

It was winter and the weather was cold. Everyone went about all muffled up in their coats, scarves, hats and mittens. 'Do your coat right up to your chin, Nicky,' called Mrs Lawson as he and the other children in the class dashed outdoors for playtime. The trees around the playground had lost their leaves long ago and looked cold and dead. The sky was grey and the wind blew in chilly gusts around the school buildings. It whipped up bits of paper, old leaves and the ends of the scarves into the air. The children had to keep moving to stay warm. Some of the girls skipped, and the boys chased. Round and round they dashed, taking turns to be 'It' and to try to catch the others.

'Here I come!' shouted Nicky and he scampered after a group of children who scattered in all directions, shrieking and laughing. 'Can't catch mee-hee!' Nicky picked out Edward to chase and set off across the playground. Round and round, nearer and nearer, closer and closer until at last, with one big leap, he grabbed Edward's jacket. 'Got you! You're "It",' he yelled.

'Oof!' puffed Edward. 'I need a rest,' and they flopped against the fence, puffing and panting. Their faces were red and they felt cosy and warm.

'That was good,' said Nicky. 'I like chasing.' They

watched the other children rushing about.

Then Edward said, 'I'm going to a new school soon.'

'Why?' asked Nicky.

'We're moving to a new house.'

'Why can't you stay at this school?'

'Because our new house is far away.' They watched the children a little longer, then Edward said suddenly, 'I'm "It" and I'm going to get you!' and he and Nicky raced off to join the others.

Two weeks later Edward was gone. He and Nicky had said goodbye and so had all the children in the class at school. Edward's mummy had given Nicky's mummy their new address and phone number, and now they were gone and there were new people living in their house. It felt a bit strange, not having Edward at school. Nicky had other friends but Edward had been his very best friend. They had played together at playgroup and at school and had tea at one another's houses and now Nicky missed Edward very much.

One day he came home from school in a bad mood. 'Whatever's the matter with you today?' asked Mummy when Nicky had shouted at Martin and thrown a cushion at Panda the cat, for no reason at all.

Nicky scowled and growled, 'We had a new teacher today and she's *horrible*!'

'Oh?' said Mummy. 'Where's Mrs Lawson?'

'Ill or something,' Nicky muttered.

'Poor Mrs Lawson.'

'Miss Nash is horrible. She shouts all the time and she said my writing was messy!'

'Well, maybe it was,' suggested Mummy.

'I don't care. I'm not doing nice work for *her*. I don't like her!' Nicky stumped off upstairs.

At breakfast next morning Nicky started to cry. 'I

51

don't want to go to school today,' he said. 'I don't like Miss Nash.'

'I'm sure she's nice really,' said Mummy. 'She's probably having to get used to you.'

'But I don't like school any more,' Nicky sniffed. 'Edward's gone and now Mrs Lawson's not there. I don't like it, it's all different.'

'Oh, deary me,' sighed Mummy and she sat down beside Nicky with her mug of morning tea. 'Changes can be a bit difficult,' she said.

'They're horrible!' said Nicky.

'Not always! You liked it when we changed the furniture round in your bedroom. You liked it when you started school.'

'Yes, but they were *nice* changes!' Nicky argued. Mummy drank her tea and Nicky poked at his soggy cornflakes with his spoon. 'Why do we have to have changes?' he sighed.

'That's just the way life is, I suppose,' said Mummy. She thought for a while. 'If we didn't have changes life would be very boring.'

'Well, why can't we have just nice changes, then?' asked Nicky, stirring his cornflakes round and round.

'Because that's how life is, lovey. Some changes are nice and some aren't. You'll make new friends and you can visit Edward in the holidays and Mrs Lawson will be back at school again soon. Anyway,' Mummy went on, 'God never changes. That's a nice thing to remember. He's the same today as he was yesterday and as he will be tomorrow. He's *always* there and he's always the same. And he's taking care of you through all the changes – the good ones and the bad ones!' Nicky smiled a little bit and nodded slowly. 'Now eat up or we'll be late,' said Mummy and she began to clear the table.

Nicky went to school, although he still didn't really want to, but somehow things were better that day. At home-time he bounced out of school as happy as could be. 'You look cheerful this afternoon,' said Mummy. 'Have you had a good day?'

'Yes!' replied Nicky with a beaming smile. 'We had a really good time. Miss Nash let us paint our feet and do foot patterns. It was great fun! Can Stefan come and play today?' So Stefan came to play at Nicky's house and they had a lovely time together.

The next morning Nicky went off happily to school. 'Miss Nash said we're going to do cooking today,' he told Mummy excitedly. 'I *like* Miss Nash!'

Nicky counts to ten

'Come on now, Danny. Eat up your dinner,' said Auntie Liz. Nicky's little cousin Daniel opened his mouth wide as Auntie Liz put in another spoonful from a dish of greeny-yellow mush. Nicky watched in horror. Danny's face seemed to be covered in green stuff and, now and then, he blew bubbles with what Auntie Liz had just spooned into his mouth. Then he would chuckle with delight as it ran down his chin and into his messy green bib. Nicky shuddered and looked away.

'What's *that*?' asked Martin, pointing at Danny's dish.

'Mixed green vegetables,' said Auntie Liz. 'Want to try some?'

'No, thanks!' replied Martin, quickly. 'It looks like caterpillar soup!'

Nicky made a face. 'Yuk! I feel sick. He's making such a *mess*.'

Auntie Liz laughed and Mummy said, 'You used to be just as messy when you were a baby.' Nicky shook his head furiously. Never! He could never have been as bad as that!

'Can I get down now?' he asked. 'I've finished.'

Mummy nodded. 'All right, you can both get down.' Nicky and Martin left the table as quickly as they could.

They liked it when Auntie Liz came for the day,

except for mealtimes. Baby Danny was so messy they couldn't enjoy their food. Martin went out into the garden and Nicky began work on a new Lego tower. He'd had the idea during lunch and he was keen to begin. He worked away busily, murmuring to himself. 'Put the long blue bricks here . . . build it up high . . . make the base strong.'

'Bub-bub-bub!' shouted Danny from the kitchen. Mummy and Auntie Liz were chatting. All was peaceful. Then Auntie Liz wiped Danny's hands and face, took off his bib and popped him on the floor. 'There you are, Bubs. Go and play with your toys.'

Pit-pat, pit-pat into the sitting-room stumped Danny, slowly and carefully, with his arms out to help him balance. He was learning to walk and he thought he was very clever. 'Dan-Dans!' he shouted and toddled over to Nicky. He grinned happily. Nicky liked when Danny did that. He looked so funny with only two teeth at the front, like a fat rabbit. Danny swayed and sat down suddenly. Then he began to empty his toy basket. Ducks, cars, balls and rattles were scattered all around him. Now and then he'd hold up something and say 'Bubb-boo!' and Nicky would smile and say 'car' or 'dog' to help him learn their real names.

The Lego tower grew and Danny became tired of his toys. He crawled across and grabbed some Lego bricks. 'Bubb-boo!' he said again.

Nicky was alarmed. 'No, Danny! Don't touch the Lego!' But Danny didn't understand. He wanted to play with Nicky. He tried to put some bricks on top of the tower. 'No, Danny!' Nicky shouted. 'Stop it!'

Mummy and Auntie Liz came in and sat down. 'Come here Bubs,' said Auntie Liz. 'You leave Nicky alone.' She held out a rusk to Danny and he pit-patted across

to get it. Nicky settled down again, but not for long!
Back came Danny, squishy rusk in one hand, to help
him build his tower. Mummy and Auntie Liz were talking again. Danny picked up more bricks.

Nicky pushed him gently. 'No, Danny, don't touch.'
But Danny took no notice. With one swipe of his fat
little hand he sent the top half of the tower flying in all
directions. Nicky lost his temper. 'No, Danny, NO!' he
shouted. 'GO AWAY!'

Up jumped Auntie Liz to rescue Danny who was
crying loudly. Up jumped Mummy to help collect the
Lego. 'It's time he had a nap,' said Auntie Liz and she
took Danny upstairs.

'Don't shout at the poor little chap. He's only a baby,'
said Mummy.

Nicky was red in the face and still cross. 'But look
what he's *done*!' he said. 'He's a nuisance, that baby!'

'You'd be safer working on the table where Danny
can't reach,' said Mummy. Eventually everything was
sorted out and Nicky went back to his tower, working
peacefully.

Later that day, when Auntie Liz and the baby had
gone home, Nicky and Martin were playing 'Donkey'.
It was a new card game that Auntie Liz had brought
them. Nicky and Martin enjoyed playing card games and
they both liked to win. Martin won the game three times
and Nicky was getting fed up. Why did Martin win so
much he wondered? Once again Nicky was left with the
Donkey card. He was sure he should have won. 'You
cheated, Martin,' he said.

Martin just grinned. 'I didn't!'

'You did!'

'Didn't!'

'Did-did-did!'

'I *didn't*!'

Nicky lost his temper again. He jumped on Martin and started to punch him. 'Boys!' shouted Mummy. 'What's going on?'

Martin was rolling about and laughing. 'Nicky said I was cheating.'

Nicky wasn't laughing. He was very cross. 'You *were* cheating, you big, fat pig!' and he punched Martin again.

Mummy pulled them apart. 'Martin, don't tease him, *please*. And Nicky, you'll have to do something about that temper of yours.'

A few days later Nicky lost his temper at school. He and Stefan were playing with some other children in the sand-pit one playtime. They were building a smuggler's cave and chatting happily. 'I got a new bike for my birthday,' said Stefan suddenly. 'It's got front and back brakes *and* reflectors!' he added impressively. Nicky scooped and patted sand as he thought. His bike was quite old. It had been Martin's before he had it. Daddy had cleaned and painted it and it *looked* new, but it wasn't.

'I've got brakes too,' he said.

'But you haven't got reflectors,' said Stefan. Nicky thought about this. He wasn't sure what reflectors were but he didn't think he had any. He was a bit annoyed about this. He was also cross at the way Stefan was talking on and on about his new bike.

'Anyway, *my* bike goes really fast!' he said at last.

Stefan wasn't impressed. 'I 'spect I can go faster. I 'spect I could go a hundred miles an hour if I wanted to.'

'Huh! I could go *three* hundred on *my* bike!' was Nicky's reply. He knew he was being silly but he was tired of Stefan showing off.

'Well, anyway, my bike's got reflectors and *yours* hasn't!' said Stefan proudly. Nicky lost his temper then and he flicked a heap of sand at Stefan's face. 'Whaaa!' yelled Stefan. 'I can't see!' A crowd of children clustered round him and bustled him off importantly to a dinner lady. She sent Stefan inside to be cleaned up and then came to find Nicky. He was in trouble again!

That afternoon Mummy had to go and see Mrs Lawson and then she and Stefan's mummy had a chat at the school gate. Everything was sorted out, but Mummy was rather solemn on the way home.

'Nicky, you must try not to lose your temper. It's getting you into trouble and that's sad.' Nicky didn't answer. He didn't like making people sad and he liked Stefan really. He also hated being told off. 'I wonder what we could do to help?' said Mummy as they set off down the road from school. While they were walking Mummy suddenly said, 'You know, I used to get into trouble with my temper when I was a little girl. I used to get *so* cross!' Nicky was surprised. He stopped in the middle of the pavement and Mummy nearly fell over him! His mummy being naughty? He found that very hard to imagine but Mummy said it was true. 'Do you know what my daddy taught me to do when someone made me cross?' Nicky shook his head. 'He said, "Always count to ten before you do or say anything".' Nicky looked puzzled.

'That's silly,' he said.

'No, it isn't,' said Mummy, 'because counting to ten gives you time to think. You can think about what to say or do. What may happen if you hit someone or shout at them?'

'They do it back,' said Nicky.

'Yes, and then that's a fight, isn't it?' Nicky nodded

slowly. 'Well, what if you *didn't* shout or hit?' asked Mummy.

Nicky thought for a moment. 'No fight?'

'That's right, no fight. If you keep quiet or only say nice things it stops a fight from beginning and *then* you don't get into trouble.'

'But Stefan was really showing off!' protested Nicky.

'Oh, I know it's not always easy. People can make us very cross. But counting to ten really does help. I still try to do it now.'

Nicky looked at Mummy. 'But you get cross sometimes,' he reminded her.

'Yes, I do,' admitted Mummy. 'But not as often as I used to and usually it's when I've forgotten to count to ten!'

Nicky smiled now. 'You try it,' said Mummy, giving him a hug. It's much better than shouting and fighting and much, *much* better than getting told off!'

So Nicky tried out the 'Count to Ten' plan. When Martin laughed at his new reading book and said it was 'easy-peasy', he counted, one, two, three, four, five, six, seven, eight, nine, TEN. . . . and just ignored him! It wasn't always easy to do and sometimes he forgot until it was too late. But, when Mummy was there to remind him, and if he tried hard, then it seemed to work and it really *did* help.

The marble bag

Plink! Plonk! Plinkity-plinkity-plinkity plonk! The big blue and silver marble rolled and bounced, rolled and bounced all the way down the stairs. Nicky scrambled after it and caught it, just as it rolled across the hall floor. He picked it up and held it to his eye. 'Caught you!' he said and then he smiled to himself as he turned it, this way and that, admiring the blue swirly pattern that twirled around in its centre. For the thousandth time he wondered how the patterns got inside the marbles. Who put them there? Was it difficult to do?

Like lots and lots of other children in his school, Nicky was collecting marbles. For a while it had been football that had kept them busy, then it was stickers, but now, without anyone really knowing why or when it had started, suddenly it was marbles. Each day in the playground little groups of children could be seen huddled around a game of marbles or busy swopping. 'I'll swop you this Galaxy for your big Oily'. 'Give me four Pee-wees for this King!'

Mummy had made Nicky a little bag to carry his marbles in – like a tiny shoe-bag – with a cord to pull the opening tight and to carry it by. Nicky had quite a lot of marbles now, all sizes and colours. Some he'd swopped, some he'd bought with his pocket money and a few he'd actually won from other children. He was very proud of his marbles and he knew each one and could tell whenever there was one missing. If a marble was lost then a great hunt began and Nicky wouldn't rest until it was found. Usually the lost marbles turned up in silly places like inside Daddy's slippers or under the fridge. Often Nicky could be found lying on the kitchen floor, poking about under the cooker or the fridge with one of Mummy's long wooden spoons, trying to reach a lost marble.

Mummy had said that she didn't want to see the marbles on the floor *any more* and especially on the stairs, but somehow they seemed to get scattered all around the house. That was when Mummy made the marble bag! Now Nicky could keep them safe and if one did escape, like the big blue and silver one, he chased after it at once and popped it back with the others, ready to take to school.

Martin had even more marbles. 'Millions and trillions!' he boasted. He kept them in an old biscuit tin that was almost too heavy to lift. Sometimes he'd take them out and count them or arrange them in sets, but he didn't take his to school. He'd given Nicky a few that he didn't need but he still had lots left. Nicky was a bit envious of Martin but he was still hopeful of winning some marbles from his friends at school.

One playtime, as the children were collecting their coats to go out, a big boy in Nicky's class, called Stuart, suddenly said, 'My marble bag's gone! Someone's taken it!' Some of the children took no notice and went on out to play but others gathered round Stuart asking questions.

'Where did you put it?'

'What does it look like?'

'Who's taken it?'

Nicky stopped to watch and listen, and he zipped up his jacket. He didn't play with Stuart much because Stuart was a bit bossy and he shouted a lot. He was shouting now and looking very fierce.

'Someone's taken it! I know they have! Someone's got *my* marble bag!'

'Who? Who? Who?' asked lots of excited voices.

'I'll find out,' said Stuart angrily.

Nicky finished doing up his coat and went out to find Stefan. They'd been happily rolling marbles and arguing about whose marble had hit whose when another boy from their class bounded up looking important. 'You're in trouble, Nicky. Stuart says you took his marble bag!' Nicky shrugged his shoulders.

'It wasn't me. I've already got one.'

'Yes, but Stuart says you took his because he saw you near his coat peg.'

'But my coat peg's next to his,' protested Nicky. 'I have to go near his peg to reach mine.'

'Well, anyway, you'd better watch out!' said the boy and off he ran again.

Nicky and Stefan went on with their game until along came Stuart and his friends. 'Hey, Nicky! Where have you put my marble bag? I *know* you took it!'

'No, I didn't,' said Nicky patiently. 'I don't *need* your bag. My Mummy's made me one.'

'Yes, he's got his own, so there!' said Stefan bravely, as he and Nicky gathered up their marbles.

'Huh!' growled Stuart and he stamped off. 'I'm telling Mrs Lawson!'

When playtime was over and the children were back in the classroom Mrs Lawson tried to sort out the problem. 'Did you take Stuart's marble bag?' she asked

Nicky. Nicky shook his head.

'No, I didn't.'

'Really?' Nicky nodded and looked very serious.

'He did! I know he did!' insisted Stuart. But when Mrs Lawson asked him more questions Stuart couldn't say how he knew or why he thought it was Nicky.

'Are you sure you're telling me the truth, Nicky?' she asked once more. Nicky was feeling a bit annoyed and impatient with Stuart by now.

'Yes,' he sighed. 'He just won't believe me.'

'Well, if you know you didn't do it then you don't need to worry. We'll find out what *really* happened to this mysterious missing marble bag sooner or later. Now let's get back to work!'

But Nicky did begin to worry. It was very upsetting when someone was blaming you for something you hadn't done, especially when that someone was bigger than you were! For the rest of the day Stuart kept muttering and giving Nicky fierce looks. Nicky started to feel very uncomfortable.

At breakfast next day Nicky suddenly said, 'I'm not going to school today.' Mummy put her hand on his forehead.

'Are you feeling all right?' she asked.

Nicky started to nod his head, then the nod changed into a shake. He shrugged and sighed. 'Well, I'm not *poorly* but I *am* worried.' Then he explained about Stuart and the lost marble bag. '. . . and I *didn't* take it, Mummy. Really and truly I didn't.'

'Well, if you didn't do it you have no need to be worried,' said Mummy.

'That's what Mrs Lawson said, but it isn't nice. Stuart keeps *looking* at me,' said Nicky sadly.

'You show me which one he is and I'll come and bash

him up!' Martin offered.

'No, I don't think that's the answer,' laughed Mummy. 'I think you'd better go to school or Stuart might think you were scared of him because you *had* taken his marbles.' Nicky nibbled his toast gloomily. 'If you have more trouble today I'll pop in and see Mrs Lawson after school.' Nicky felt a bit better then and finished his breakfast.

Just before they left for school Mummy had a good idea. She said, 'Let's just tell God about all this. He likes us to tell him our worries.' So they did, and then they had to hurry before they were late.

After assembly Mrs Lawson asked Stuart, 'Has that marble bag appeared yet?'

'No,' he replied, giving Nicky another fierce look.

'Well, I've decided that this classroom needs a spring-clean! So, when you've finished your number work you can all help me tidy it up and maybe we'll solve the mystery of the missing marble bag!' So, as the children finished their work they started to sort puzzles, tidy piles of books, sweep behind cupboards and fold dressing-up clothes. The classroom began to look very tidy and the waste paper bin had to be emptied *four* times!

It was nearly playtime when Charlene called out, 'Look! Here it is!' and held up a marble bag. It had been underneath the cover of the sand tray all the time!

'Oh, well done, Charlene!' said Mrs Lawson with a beaming smile. Then she turned to Stuart. 'Is it yours, Stuart?' Stuart nodded. 'Were you playing in the sand tray yesterday?' Stuart nodded again. 'Hmmm!' said Mrs Lawson and she gave him a long look. Stuart shuffled his feet and his ears went pink. 'I think,' said Mrs Lawson rather sternly, 'that you should say sorry to Nicky for what you said yesterday.' So, there in front of all the children, Stuart had to apologise to Nicky for saying he'd taken the marble bag.

Nicky was hardly listening, he was so pleased and very relieved. Now everyone *knew* he'd been telling the truth and he didn't need to worry any more. When Mummy collected him from school that afternoon she could tell by Nicky's happy, smiling face that everything was all right now.

'There you are!' she said. 'You knew you were telling the truth and God knew you were too. We told him all about it and he looked after you, didn't he?' Nicky grinned and bounced up and down happily, twirling his marble bag by its cord.

'Come on,' said Mummy. 'Let's go and collect Martin and then we'll buy some buns to celebrate!'

Nicky plays the recorder

Toot-toot, toot-toot, tootle – *squeak!* 'Oops!' Toot-toot, *squawk*-toot . . . ! 'Oh, *bother!*'

Nicky was learning to play his new recorder and it wasn't very easy. It had been a Christmas present and, for a while, it had stayed in its box, but now, suddenly, Nicky wanted to learn to play it. Mummy had shown him where to put his fingers and he'd practised and practised and now he could almost play 'Twinkle, twinkle, little star.' Now and again an odd squeak or squawk came in when it shouldn't but, if you listened hard, you could hear the tune at last.

Nicky kept trying. He played in bed, he played in the bath, he played in the garden. He even tried playing at mealtimes, but nobody else liked that idea very much!

At last he felt he could play it just right. He went to find someone to listen to him. He found Daddy in the back garden.

'Daddy, listen to this!' He began to play. Toot-toot, toot-toot, tootle . . . But Daddy was busy.

'Not just now, Nick. Let me get this grass cut first.' He started the mower with a roar that made Nicky's ears buzz. Nicky sighed and went back indoors. There he could hear Mummy's voice from the hall.

'Listen, Mummy!' he called and he started to play

again. Toot-toot, toot-too . . . !

Mummy was talking on the phone. 'Shhh!' She made a cross face and waved Nicky away. Oh dear, didn't anyone want to hear him play?

Crash-thump! Down the stairs came Martin, in a great hurry. 'Listen to me playing,' Nicky began.

'Sorry, can't stop now! I'm late for football practice. I'll listen later!' and away he ran.

Nicky sat on the bottom stair and frowned at the front door which Martin had just slammed behind him. He could hear the roar of the mower from the garden, and Mummy *still* talking on the phone. There *must* be someone who would like to hear him play his tune. Then he spied Panda the cat, curled up on a chair in the sitting room. 'Perhaps she'd like to hear me play,' thought Nicky. But after only three toots Panda's ears went twitch-twitch! She jumped off the chair and stalked out of the room with her tail up high.

Well, that was that. There was no one left to listen now. Nicky felt sad and a bit annoyed. Everyone seemed to be too busy. No one had time to listen to him. He wandered out of the house and down the back garden to the shed. This was the place where he did his digging and a lot of his thinking. It was his special spot. He sat down on the big up-turned flowerpot that stood near his digging patch and gave a thoughtful little toot on his recorder. He was still and quiet for a while, then he smiled to himself.

As Daddy pushed the lawn mower back to the shed he heard something that made him stop and listen. Toot-toot, toot-toot, tootle-toot! He followed the sound and found Nicky sitting all alone on his flowerpot, happily playing 'Twinkle, twinkle, little star' on his recorder. When he'd finished Daddy clapped loudly and Nicky

nearly fell off his flowerpot in surprise!

'That was *very* good, Nicky!' said Daddy. 'But what are you doing up here all alone?' Nicky shrugged his shoulders.

'Well, everyone seemed to be too busy to listen to me. You were cutting the grass, Mummy's talking on the phone, Martin's gone to football and Panda just walks away. Then I remembered how you said that God is always with us, so I thought well, maybe *he* would listen to me!'

Daddy nodded and smiled. 'You were quite right. God *is* always with us and he always has time for us. I'm sure he has been listening and enjoying your playing. I'm sorry we were all too busy to listen, because you're playing so nicely. Come and play for Mummy and me now. I promise we'll listen properly this time!' So Nicky and Daddy went back down the garden and they had a special performance of 'Twinkle, twinkle, little star' in the kitchen with *no* mistakes. When he'd finished, Mummy and Daddy clapped, and Nicky's cheeks went pink with pleasure.

'That was lovely,' said Mummy. 'I like your playing very much.'

Daddy laughed and pointed. 'I'm afraid there's some-one who still doesn't enjoy your playing!' And there was Panda, with twitching ears, hurrying out of the kitchen with her tail up high!

The bedroom wolf

'Mummy! Mummy! Mummeee!' It was the middle of the night and Nicky was sitting up in bed crying. There was a thud and a bump as Mummy hurried into the bedroom.

'What's the matter, Nicky? Do you feel sick?' she asked anxiously. Nicky was shivering and his eyes were staring.

'Mummy.'

'What is it?'

'Mummy, it was over there.' Nicky pointed to the corner of the room. Mummy stared into the shadows.

'What was, lovey?'

'The wolf, Mummy.' Nicky shuddered and hid his face in Mummy's shoulder. Mummy laughed.

'There's no wolf in here. You've had a bad dream.'

But there *was* a wolf here, thought Nicky. It's gone now, though.

There was a creaking and a grunting from the top bunk and Martin turned over.

'What's the noise?' he asked sleepily.

'It's all right,' said Mummy. 'Nicky had a bad dream.'

'It was a wolf,' said Nicky, a bit more bravely now.

'Huh!' muttered Martin. 'There aren't any wolves round here!' and he went back to sleep.

'There you are,' said Mummy. 'Now, off you go to sleep and don't worry any more.' For a few minutes she sat beside Nicky until he was asleep again.

In the morning Nicky had almost forgotten about the bad dream and during the day at school he didn't think about it at all. But at bedtime he started to feel worried. The bedroom seemed different at night-time. Even with the night-light, which was on all night, there were strange shadows and shapes that weren't there in the day-time. 'Mummy, don't go downstairs,' said Nicky when story and prayers were finished.

'Why not, Nicky?' asked Mummy.

'I'm worried about the wolf,' and he began to cry.

'There *is* no wolf,' said Mummy patiently. 'Come and see!' and together they went all round the bedroom. 'You see?' said Mummy when Nicky was tucked up in bed again. 'No wolf, right?'

'Mmmm,' Nicky nodded, feeling a bit silly.

'Now off you go to sleep. Night night.'

Soon Nicky was asleep but, in the middle of the night, he had another bad dream. This time Daddy came and, after a little chat, Nicky settled down again. The next night was the same and the next, and the next, and the next. Sometimes Mummy got up, sometimes Daddy got up but each night it was the same old wolf and poor Nicky was always frightened.

On Saturday morning at breakfast Daddy said, 'I'm tired of this wolf business. We'll have to do something about it.'

Nicky stared into his cornflakes and said nothing. The wolf never seemed worrying in the day-time, but night-time was different! Later, while Nicky and Martin were out in the garden, Mummy and Daddy got busy with a plan.

After tea that evening Mummy announced, 'We're going to play a game before you go to bed, Nicky. We're going on a wolf hunt!'

Nicky looked puzzled but Martin seemed excited. 'Great!' he shouted. 'I'll get a big stick!'

'What's going on?' wondered Nicky. He soon found out! Mummy and Daddy, Nicky and Martin went all round the house, looking into cupboards and under beds. Behind the settee and in the toy-box. At last Daddy shouted, 'Ah-ha! Gotcha!' and he pulled a big cardboard shape out from behind the dressing-table in the boys' bedroom. The shape was a wolf! It was a clever drawing with big, fierce eyes, a bushy tail, a red mouth and huge, sharp teeth. Nicky stepped back and watched while Martin grabbed the cardboard wolf and whacked it with his stick. 'Come on, Nick!' he shouted, 'Come and whack the wolf!'

Nicky wasn't sure at first but eventually he joined in and jumped on the cardboard until it began to fall to pieces. Then the whole family paraded downstairs, out of the back door and the tattered wolf shape was dropped into the dustbin.

'That was good fun,' said Martin. Nicky nodded slowly but he didn't say anything.

When he was in bed Mummy came to say prayers with him. 'Do you remember that Sunday School song that says "My God is so great, so strong and so mighty. There's nothing my God cannot do"?' Nicky remembered all right. It was one of his favourites. 'Well, let's ask God to take away the bad dreams. He's so strong and mighty that it'll be an easy thing for him to do!' So Nicky and Mummy told God about the wolf and asked him to keep the bad dreams away and help Nicky to be brave.

That night the wolf didn't come. Everyone was very pleased the next morning. After that they played the wolf hunt game every night, and each time, they found another cardboard wolf shape! Sometimes the wolf was under a bed, sometimes he was behind the fridge but every night a cardboard wolf ended up in pieces in the dustbin. Sometimes Nicky still had a bad dream but not very often. Soon he had almost forgotten about the wolf. One night, as the family got ready for the wolf-hunt Nicky sighed and said, 'This is a silly game. Do we *have* to play it? I'm tired!' and off he went to bed.

From then on, if ever Nicky was worried about something Mummy and Daddy reminded him about the 'so strong and so mighty' song and then they asked God to help.

And the wolf never, ever visited them again.

Nicky and the big red tulip

'But I *want* Stefan to come and play!' It was home-time and all the school children were streaming out of the playground. Nicky and Mummy stood with the other mothers and children at the school gates. Nicky and his friend Stefan had made a plan at school. Stefan was going to come and play at Nicky's house and they were going to start work on another new, very big hole by the garden shed. They would maybe find treasure or fossils or something else really exciting. They had it all organised and now Mummy said they couldn't do it. Nicky's bottom lip went out, as it usually did when he was cross. His eyebrows looked very fierce and wrinkled-up and he kicked at a stone on the path. 'Why can't Stefan come?'

'He's got to go to the dentist,' Mummy explained.

''Fraid so, Nicky,' said Stefan's mummy. 'I'm sure Stefan would *much* rather come and play with you but we can't miss his check-up, it's important.'

'We'll arrange another day,' said Mummy, trying to cheer Nicky up, but he didn't want to cheer up, he wanted to play with Stefan!

Nicky sulked all the way home and wouldn't speak to anyone. Martin tried to tell him about a project on wild animals that his class was doing but Nicky only grunted and humphed and wouldn't be interested. Mummy tried chatting about this and that, just to help Nicky to forget about being grumpy, but it didn't work.

They arrived home and, as soon as she got indoors, Mummy put the kettle on. Nicky stayed out on the back doorstep, scowling and staring angrily at the garden. By the back door was a very big flowerpot that Mummy had planted with spring bulbs. There had been daffodils there, but they were finished now and only the green leaves were left. But in the middle were three tulips. Two of them had tight, greeny-yellow flower buds but, for some reason, the third bulb was already in full flower. It was a lovely, bright red, shiny tulip, with a black and yellow centre. It stood up tall and straight amongst all the green stalks and leaves, like a big red lollipop. It nodded slightly in the breeze and seemed to be talking to him. 'Cheer up, Nicky. It's not so bad,' but still Nicky sat and frowned.

He heard Mummy clattering in the kitchen. 'I want a drink!' he growled, as he came indoors.

Mummy's eyebrows went up and seemed to say, 'Pardon?'

'I want a *drink*!' Nicky repeated more loudly.

'I heard you, Nicky,' Mummy replied calmly. 'I'm just waiting for something else.'

There was a pause . . . 'Please,' said Nicky at last. Mummy smiled and handed him a mug of orange.

'Biscuit?' she asked.

'Yes . . . please.' Mummy gave him the biscuit jar and he peered inside. 'Where are the chocolate ones?' he asked.

'I'm keeping those for visitors. I want to use up these first,' Mummy replied.

'I don't *like* these. I want a chocolate one!' Mummy shut her eyes for a moment and seemed to be breathing

rather carefully.

'Sorry, no chocolate biscuits today, Nicky.'

'Give me one!'

'No!'

'Yes!'

'NO!' Mummy was cross now, Nicky could see that, but he was too angry to care. He slammed down his mug and the orange slopped on the table. Then he stamped out into the garden.

'I hate you!' he shouted. 'You're horrible!' Then, almost before he knew what had happened, he'd grabbed the smooth, straight stalk of the red tulip and snapped it off. Then he flung the flower on the path and stamped on it, crying and shouting at the same time, 'I hate you, hate you, hate you!'

It was very quiet after that and then Nicky found Mummy standing beside him and he saw Martin's worried face peering out from the doorway. He looked at the crushed and broken petals on the ground and then he cried properly, because now he was sad and very, very sorry. Mummy cuddled him while he cried but she didn't say anything. 'Mend it, Mummy! Mend it!' he sobbed.

'I can't mend it, lovey,' said Mummy quietly. Nicky rubbed his eyes and looked at Mummy. Then he saw that she had tears on her face too.

'Don't cry about the flower, Mummy,' he pleaded.

Mummy smiled. 'I'm not crying for the flower, Nicky,' and she hugged him very tight.

Nicky was still sad. He hadn't meant to spoil the tulip and make Mummy upset. It all just seemed to happen when he was so cross. Now the flower was gone and he couldn't bring it back. He'd spoiled it for everyone. He looked at the broken stem in the flowerpot and began to cry again. 'I'm sorry I broke your flower,' he said at last.

'Cheer up,' said Mummy as she wiped his smudgy face. 'It'll grow again next year. Just remember, though, next time you're cross, go and punch your pillow or dig hard in your big hole down the garden and then nothing will be spoiled and no one will be sad. Now, come and help me crack the eggs for the cake I'm making. You're good at that, aren't you?'

A few days later the other tulips in Mummy's flowerpot opened their buds. They were yellow with red stripes. They were pretty and cheerful but not as nice as the big red one. It was a long time before Nicky could look at the flowerpot without feeling sad.

Now it's springtime again and Nicky has been watching carefully as the tulip leaves push their way through the soil in Mummy's big flowerpot. The big red tulip is there again – first in flower - shining brightly for everyone to enjoy, and Nicky is looking after it very carefully!

When Mummy was ill

'Where's Mummy?' asked Nicky, one Saturday morning. It was breakfast-time and Daddy was in the kitchen, but there was no sign of Mummy.

'Mummy's not feeling very well,' said Daddy. 'She's staying in bed.'

'What's wrong with her?' asked Nicky.

'Sore throat and a headache,' Daddy replied. 'She's been feeling poorly for a few days and I think she needs to stay in bed today.'

'What about breakfast?' was Nicky's next question.

'I'm doing it,' said Daddy. 'What do you want?'

'Weetabix with *warm* milk and a boiled egg,' came the quick reply as Nicky sat down at the table. Daddy looked at him doubtfully.

'Do you *usually* have a boiled egg?'

'Quite often,' said Nicky. 'Mummy says they're good for us.'

Martin bounced in. 'Where's Mum?'

'She's got a sore throat,' Nicky announced. 'She's in bed.'

'What about breakfast?'

'Daddy's doing it.'

'Oh!'

The boys watched while Daddy set the table and found

83

pans for milk and eggs.

'I want porridge,' said Martin.

'Sorry, no porridge,' said Daddy.

'Why?'

'Because I can't make it, that's why!' Daddy replied firmly.

'But Mummy knows,' grumbled Martin. 'Why can't *she* do it?'

'She's not well,' Nicky reminded him.

'Huh!' Martin made a face.

For a while Daddy was busy with milk and the kettle and the teapot and boxes of cereal. Nicky sighed. 'Daddy, I want my breakfast.'

'All right, it's coming,' muttered Daddy.

'It's taking a *long* time,' said Martin, grumbling.

'Well, how about doing something to help?' Daddy replied rather crossly. 'You do the toast, Martin, and, Nicky, put cereal in the bowls.'

Martin put two slices of bread in the toaster and pushed the lever down while Nicky struggled with a big box of cereal. Very soon breakfast was ready. The toast was all right, but Nicky was annoyed when his milk was too hot, and very cross when he discovered his egg was hard. 'Mummy doesn't do it like this,' he grumbled. 'Why can't Mummy do it?' Daddy sighed and went upstairs with a cup of tea for Mummy.

After breakfast Nicky wandered upstairs to find Mummy. The bedroom was gloomy because the curtains were still closed. Nicky patted the hump of bedclothes on Mummy's side of the bed.

'Uh!' said a croaky voice.

'Mummy.'

'Ooh, Nicky. You woke me up!' This croaky, squeaky voice didn't sound like Mummy . . . but it was!

'Mummy, get up!' said Nicky sternly. 'I want you.'

'Later, lovey,' Mummy croaked. 'I've got *such* a sore head. I'll have a little rest and then I'll get up.'

'But I *need* you!'

'Daddy's here, he'll help you,' said Mummy in a squeaky whisper. Daddy came in just then and told Nicky to leave Mummy alone. Nicky didn't want to go, but he had to.

He and Daddy went to find some clothes for him to wear. Martin was in their bedroom feeling grumpy because his favourite tracksuit wasn't ironed. 'Why can't Mum do it? I want to wear it and it's all creased!'

'I don't like these socks!' wailed Nicky. Daddy sat down on Nicky's bottom bunk and shook his head.

'Boys, this just *won't* do,' he said. 'Mummy really doesn't feel well. She isn't pretending, you know. She'll feel worse if she hears us moaning and groaning. We're all fed up, but let's think about Mummy. She's the one who's ill. If we think about her it will stop us feeling sorry for ourselves. Now what can we do to help Mummy?'

The boys sat and thought. 'Get some medicine?' suggested Martin.

'Yes, we could get something when we do the shopping,' agreed Daddy. 'But what else?'

'Read her a story?' said Nicky.

'Well, maybe later when her head's better,' Daddy agreed. 'The best thing we could all do would be to cheer up.' The boys agreed. Moaning and groaning hadn't made things any better, so perhaps being cheerful would help. Nicky went to wash himself and Martin tidied the bunk-beds, while Daddy quickly swished the iron over the crumpled tracksuit.

Soon they were both dressed and busy downstairs,

clearing the breakfast things and tidying up. Later they went out with Daddy to the shops, 'To give Mummy some peace and quiet,' said Daddy. They bought the usual things like bread and potatoes and then they got some extra-strong throat sweets that the chemist said were very good. They also bought some special treats like chocolate biscuits and comics and soon they all felt much happier. When they got home Nicky found the kitchen scissors and then he went and cut some flowers from the garden which Martin helped him to arrange. They put these with some soup and the throat sweets on Mummy's lunch tray.

This time when they went upstairs the curtains were open and the bedroom was bright and sunny. Mummy was sitting up and smiling. 'Oh, what lovely flowers,' she said, still in her croaky voice.

'Are you better now?' asked Nicky anxiously.

'*Much* better, thank you. My headache's gone and my throat isn't so sore now, just croaky.' Nicky was pleased and he bounced on the bed.

'Careful!' warned Daddy. 'If you spill the soup on the bed we'll have to learn how to use the washing machine!' They all laughed and Nicky felt very happy.

'Later on, I'm going to read you a story,' he promised. 'Me and Martin have to help Daddy make our lunch first. Don't go to sleep, will you?'

'No, I promise!' laughed Mummy, 'and thank you for being such helpful boys.'

The picnic

'Bang!' The front door slammed and Nicky jumped up. 'Daddy's home!' He and Martin dashed into the hall and there, sure enough, was Daddy.

'Hello, boys,' he said, giving them a hug. 'Where's Mummy?'

'Here I am!' came a voice from upstairs and then Mummy came hurrying down, looking very happy. Daddy's work had sent him away for nearly a week and everyone was glad to have him home again.

While tea was cooking Nicky showed Daddy his new reading book and Martin told him three new 'Knock-knock' jokes that he'd learnt. Then Daddy rummaged through his suitcase and the boys hovered around hopefully. At last he found a little car for Nicky and a book about dinosaurs for Martin.

Tea was a happy meal because it was good to be together again. Daddy had been very busy for a long time and he'd been away such a lot. Nicky missed Daddy when he was away. True, all the usual things happened in their usual ways but somehow it felt different when Daddy wasn't there. But now Daddy was back and Nicky felt like he did when he'd just fitted the last piece into a rather difficult jigsaw puzzle. Everything felt just *right* now.

The special job that Daddy had been working on was all finished now. 'At last!' sighed Mummy.

Daddy yawned. 'I need a rest! I think I'll take some time off.'

'Holiday?' asked Nicky.

'That's right. If I don't see more of you all, I'll forget what you look like!'

So Daddy took some holiday and stayed home from work. Nicky was pleased because Daddy was there at breakfast and at tea-time every day. He sometimes took them to school or met them at the end of the day. Nicky felt very proud when Daddy met him. 'That's *my* Daddy,' he told his friends.

One evening Daddy said, 'Let's go out for the day on Saturday – somewhere special.'

'Yeees!' shouted the boys. Mummy thought it was a good idea too. After a discussion they decided to go to the sea and spend the day on the beach. The boys made plans.

'I'm going to dig,' said Nicky.

'I'm going to look for crabs,' said Martin.

'Can we have a picnic?'

'Can we go in the sea?'

'Can we play football?'

'Yes! Yes! Yes!' laughed Daddy.

On Saturday morning the whole family was up early. Nicky didn't eat much breakfast because he was too excited. Mummy was busy filling plastic boxes with sandwiches, cake and all the other things that make a picnic. Daddy was filling bottles of orange drink and making a flask of coffee. Martin was dashing up and down the stairs collecting things that he thought he might need. Soon the hall was so cluttered up with things that when Daddy went out to the car he could hardly get the front door open!

'Look, we're only going for a day, not a week, you know!' said Daddy.

It took a long time to pack everything into the car and Martin was a bit disappointed when he wasn't allowed to take his roller skates, but eventually they were ready. The journey to the sea seemed to take a long, long time. First it was stop-start, stop-start at all the traffic-lights through town. When they left the town behind and it was Mummy's turn to drive there always seemed to be a slow lorry or caravan in front of them. 'Are we nearly there yet?' Nicky kept asking.

'Not far now,' said Mummy at last and by the time Nicky had counted twenty-three yellow cars and Martin had spotted four car transporters they *were* nearly there.

'Let's find a quiet spot,' said Daddy when they'd parked the car. 'There seem to be a lot of people here already.' Getting down to the beach wasn't easy – there was so much to carry!

'Do we *really* need all this?' sighed Daddy as they set off along the path through the sand dunes. Nicky and Martin scampered along in front, dropping a bag here and tripping over a football there and although they had to keep coming back to pick up things, they didn't really mind because it was all good fun.

Although the car-park had been quite full the beach wasn't crowded and it was easy to find a quiet place on the thick, dry sand at the foot of the sand dunes. Mummy spread out a rug and Daddy put up the deck-chairs. 'Is it lunch-time?' asked Martin hopefully.

'Almost,' said Mummy. 'Take a biscuit and go and play for a while.'

'Come and have a kick-around,' said Daddy. Off they ran, down through the thick, dry sand and on to the firm, wet sand that the sea covered every day when the tide came in. Up and down, back and fooorth they ran, chasing the football this way and that. Daddy and Martin could run fast and do clever passes and tackling, and soon Nicky got left behind. He didn't really mind. After all, he could play football any time; it was the sea he wanted to look at.

It seemed a long way to the sea and, as he trotted along the sand, Nicky wondered if it was running away from him. It's teasing me, he thought, but soon his feet were splashing in shallow water. The waves were small, hardly *real* waves at all. Little ripples ran to and fro, with tiny pieces of red and green seaweed floating in them, across the crinkly-patterned sand. Nicky hopped back quickly as a bigger wave ran towards him. He pulled off his trainers and socks and tip-toed into the water. 'Oooh! It's cold!' he gasped. The waves washed to and fro, pulling the wet sand from under his heels until he felt he might fall over. His feet weren't so cold now and he splashed along in the shallow water, flicking the water with his toes and watching it fall in sparkling drops. A sea-gull swooped over his head. 'Ha-ha-ha-ha-ha!' it called.

'Who are you laughing at?' shouted Nicky. A dog galloped by, his big paws throwing up little spurts of sand and water behind him. He was chasing the sea-gull. 'You'll never catch it!' Nicky called, and splashed on.

'Nick-eee!' came a faint, faraway cry. Nicky turned and saw, far back along the beach, Daddy standing waving. Suddenly he wanted to be with the others again so he galloped, like the seagull-chasing dog, back to the sand dunes and Daddy and Mummy and Martin.

Lunch was lovely. All the ordinary things they ate at home tasted different on the beach, with the sounds of

the waves and the seagulls, and with the soft sand trickling through their toes.

'Aah! Time for a snooze!' said Daddy and he settled back in his chair.

'*I* don't want a sleep,' said Nicky, so he and Martin grabbed buckets and spades and set to work on a sand castle.

'Not *too* near, boys,' warned Mummy as a shower of sand landed in her lap. The boys worked furiously. They dug and patted, scooped and smoothed and the pile of sand grew bigger. Mummy and Daddy joined them later and they dug and patted, scooped and smoothed too, while Nicky searched for shells and pretty stones to decorate their castle.

It was hard to know when to stop. Was a sand-castle ever really finished? At last their tired arms told them to stop. Mummy took a photo of Nicky and Martin beside their castle while Daddy went to buy ice-creams.

The day passed quickly, there was so much to do. Quite suddenly, it seemed to Nicky, the beach looked different. What could have happened? Then he saw that there was more sea and less sand – the tide was coming in. Also, the sun had moved too. It was lower in the sky and a dark yellow colour. Long, black shadows stretched back from the figures on the sand. Mummy began to pack the bags. 'Time to go,' said Daddy, as he shook out the rug.

'Oooh!' said Nicky in a moany voice, but he didn't *really* mind because he felt quite tired and there was a chilly wind blowing. Back through the sand dunes they went, Daddy at the end of the procession picking up the things that were dropped.

Nicky felt *very* tired in the car as they drove away from the sea. He didn't want to talk at all, just listened to the sounds around him and thought about all that he'd done that day. The car engine hummed in a comfortable way. His face felt warm from the sunshine and his toes wriggled happily inside his sandy trainers.

'Take-away for tea tonight,' he heard Mummy's voice say.

'Mmmmm-mmmm-mmm' went the car.

'I've counted three petrol tankers already,' said Martin's voice from very far away.

Nicky's head slid sideways on to the big picnic box beside him. It's nice having Daddy back, he thought. I hope we can all come here again.

'Mmmmm-mmmm-mmm' went the car. Nicky's eyelids drooped. It's been a good day. A . . . very . . . good . . . day. . . .